THE SICK COW

Story by
H. E. TODD

Pictures by
VAL BIRO

HODDER AND STOUGHTON
LONDON SYDNEY AUCKLAND TORONTO

One day Bobby Brewster was going round the
farm with the farmer when they saw a cow
sitting in the middle of a field looking
very sorry for herself.

The farmer said, "Good morning, cow,"
and the cow looked up and said,
"Bow-wow."
"I beg your pardon?" said the farmer.
"Bow-wow," repeated the cow.

They didn't want to
hurt the cow's feelings,
so they went back to the
farm, and the farmer said
to Bobby Brewster, "Did you hear
what I heard?" and Bobby replied,
"I thought I heard the cow say 'Bow-wow'."
"It seems a very funny thing to me," said the farmer.
"I think we had better give her some medicine."

So they went to the barn and they fetched a big bottle full of horrid looking yellow stuff and a large spoon and took it back to the cow.

But the cow wouldn't
even open her mouth,
except to say "Bow-wow".
They tried to push the
spoon in between the
"Bow" and the "Wow",
but it was no good.

"We shall have to send for a cow doctor," said the farmer. Luckily, the cow doctor didn't live far away. He soon arrived carrying a little black bag, and the cow doctor, the farmer and Bobby Brewster, all went across the field to the cow. By now the cow was looking worse.

"What's the matter with you, cow?" asked the cow doctor. "Bow-wow," said the cow. "I beg your pardon?" said the cow doctor. "Bow-wow," repeated the cow. "A clear case of dog's disease," said the cow doctor. "I shall have to give her a dog's disease pill."

The cow doctor was very clever. He took a long tube and put a large white pill in one end. Then the farmer held the cow's mouth open wide and the cow doctor blew the pill, woof, down into the cow's tummy. The cow sat down and went to sleep. "We'll leave her quiet and comfortable," said the cow doctor, "and I'll come and see her again in the morning."

The next morning, the cow was
looking worse still. "How do
you feel this morning, cow?"
asked the cow doctor. The cow
looked up and said, "Miaow."
"I beg your pardon?"
said the cow doctor.
"Miaow," repeated the cow.

"Yesterday she had dog's disease, so I gave her
a dog's disease pill," said the cow doctor.
"Now she has cat's disease. This is beyond me.
We shall have to send for a cow specialist."

The cow specialist was a famous man. He lived across the sea in a place called Vienna, which is the capital of Austria. He came by helicopter, and landed the very next morning in the middle of the very next field to where the cow was.

He strode across the field followed by the cow doctor, the farmer and Bobby Brewster.

"How now cow?" he asked. The cow looked up and said "Quack! Quack!" The cow specialist took no notice. "Get up," he said sternly. The cow didn't like being spoken to like that, but she got up. "Now run round the field," demanded the cow specialist.

The very last thing the cow wanted to do was run round a field, but she ran and just when she was in the middle of a large clump of tall, very prickly thistles, the cow specialist shouted, "Sit down."

MOO!

The cow sat plonk in the
middle of the thistles,
and "MOO!" She jumped
ten feet in the air.

"What did you say?" said the cow specialist. "MOO," said the cow. "Repeat that," said the cow specialist. "MOO," repeated the cow. And from that day to this that cow has never said anything but "Moo," which all goes to prove what a very clever cow specialist that cow specialist was.

Of course, the farmer was delighted, and he invited
the cow doctor, the cow specialist and Bobby Brewster
home to the farm for tea.

ISBN 0-340-18675-5

Text copyright © H. E. Todd 1974
Illustrations copyright © Val Biro 1974

First published 1954 in *Bobby Brewster*
This edition first published 1974
Fifth impression 1982

Published by Hodder and Stoughton Children's Books,
a division of Hodder and Stoughton Ltd,
Mill Road, Dunton Green, Sevenoaks, Kent TN13 2YJ.

Printed in Great Britain by Springbourne Press,
Basildon, Essex.